what can you do with a rock?

New York Times bestselling author
PAT ZIETLOW MILLER

Illustrated by **KATIE KATH**

sourcebooks
jabberwocky

To Sonia—again!
        —PZM

To Dad, who showed me the rocks
of the land. Also, to Dr. Bollinger,
who showed me the rocks of the sea.
        —KK

Some people don't notice rocks.

They walk by, head in the air, hands in their pockets, missing the magic underfoot.

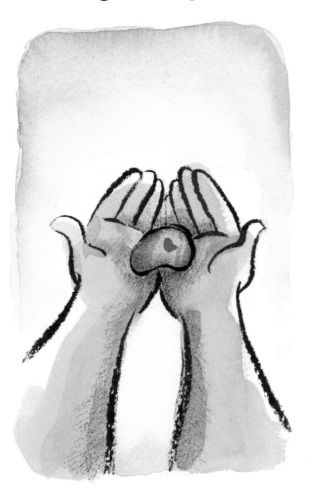

Other people see those
remarkable rocks.
And appreciate them.
After all, you can do a
lot with a rock.

YOU CAN KICK IT.
Off your porch,

down your driveway,
around the block.

Notice how it hops in
front of you, showing
you where to go.

YOU CAN SKIP IT.
First, find a flat, thin rock.
Next, find a pond or stream.
Then, flick your wrist,
hold your breath, and hope.

Your first tries might sink straight to the bottom.
But—eventually—your rock will skip.

YOU CAN DROP IT.

How many sounds can your rock make?
It's fun to find out.
But always look before you let go.

No one wants to get hit by a rock.

To really have fun with rocks, you need more than one.
Fortunately, you can find more.

From a beach,

the woods,

or your driveway.

Some rocks are for
anyone to take.
Others need to stay
where they are.

So take the rocks you can.
Admire those you can't.
And know this:
There will always
be more rocks
to see.

Once you have a pile of rocks,
you can do so much more.
YOU CAN SORT THEM.

By their color,

shape,

size,

or how they make you feel.

Should your tiny white rock go with other *tiny* rocks?
With other *white* rocks?
Or with other rocks that make you *smile*?
Only you can decide.

YOU CAN STUDY THEM.

In a museum, your school, or a wide-open field. Rocks show where glaciers traveled, when volcanoes roared, and what plants or animals lived long ago.

Want to conduct an experiment?
See how many rocks you can stack
on your hand or your knee.

Love your rocks.

Listen to them.

Learn their stories.

YOU CAN CHANGE THEM.

You can build bridges with rocks.
Or make a beautiful mosaic,
piece by perfect piece.

You even can decorate
yourself with rocks.
By making a necklace.
Or a ring.
Want to really rock the boat?
Turn your rocks into frogs,
fish, or fairies.

All you need is your imagination.

YOU CAN KEEP THEM.

Some rocks are perfect.
Maybe they remind you of somewhere.
Or fit your hand just right.
They calm you when you're scared,
and wait patiently while you think.
Don't kick, skip, or drop those rocks.
Keep them close by.

BEST OF ALL, YOU CAN SHARE THEM.

Tell someone about your perfect rock.

Explain where you found it.

How long you've had it.

Why you like it.

Then, let that person tell you about their best rock.

This might take a while.

Choose your friend carefully.
People are like rocks.
Some sparkle right away,
while others seem ordinary at first,
but have treasure deep inside.

Don't miss their magic.
Don't walk by with your head in the
air and your hands in your pockets.
Hear your friend's story.
Share yours.

And then, find some more rocks
and make new stories...together.

YOU CAN DO A LOT WITH A ROCK!

If you want to learn more about rocks, check out the information below.

KNOW HOW YOUR ROCKS WERE MADE

There are three main types of rocks. They are named by how the rocks are formed.

IGNEOUS

These rocks form when melted rock cools and hardens. This melted rock is called magma when it's inside the Earth and lava when it's on the Earth's surface. Granite, pumice and obsidian are examples of igneous rocks.

SEDIMENTARY

These rocks form from layers of sand, silt, shells, or plants. Shale, sandstone, and limestone are examples of sedimentary rocks.

METAMORPHIC

These rocks are made from other rocks that change with heat and pressure underground. Slate, marble and gneiss are examples of metamorphic rocks.

KEEP YOUR ROCKS ORGANIZED

If you like rocks, you might want to start a rock collection. There are many ways to do this.
If you want to keep it simple, you can:

- **Gather rocks you like.** But remember: If you're in a national or state park or on private property, it may be against the law to take rocks home—no matter how much you like them.

- **Keep those rocks safe.** Store them in a box, a bag, a jar, or an egg carton. Or line them up on your floor or windowsill.

- **Admire them.** Sort them. Enjoy them.

IF YOU WANT TO BE A BIT MORE OFFICIAL, YOU CAN:

- **Do some research.** Learn more about which rocks are common where you live. Find the *Roadside Geology* book for your state to get started.

- **Identify those rocks.** Use one of the nonfiction books listed below.

- **Label them.** Write each rock's name and the date and spot you found it on tape or a piece of paper that you keep by that rock. You also can record information about each of your rocks in a logbook like a geologist would.

- **Join a "rock group."** Check out Future Rockhounds of America—amfed.org/kids.htm— or a local rock and mineral club.

LEARN MORE ABOUT YOUR ROCKS

Want to learn more about how to collect, identify, catalog, and display your rocks? Or read more stories about rocks? Check out these books!

Nonfiction

- Aston, Dianna Hutts. *A Rock Is Lively*. San Francisco: Chronicle Books, 2012.
- Callery, Sean and Smith, Miranda. *Rocks, Minerals & Gems*. New York: Scholastic, 2016.
- Hurst, Carol Otis. *Rocks In His Head*. New York: Greenwillow Books, 2001.
- Lewis, Gary. *My Awesome Field Guide to Rocks and Minerals: Track and Identify Your Treasures*. New York: Rockridge Press, 2019.
- Lynch, Dan R. *Rock Collecting for Kids*. Cambridge, Minnesota: Adventure Publications, 2018.
- Tomecek, Steve. *Everything Rocks and Minerals*. Washington, DC: National Geographic Kids Books, 2011.

Fiction

- Baylor, Byrd. *Everybody Needs a Rock*. New York: Aladdin Paperbacks, 1974.
- Christian, Peggy. *If You Find a Rock*. Boston: Houghton Mifflin Harcourt, 2000.
- Griffin, Molly Beth. *Rhoda's Rock Hunt*. St. Paul: Minnesota Historical Society Press, 2014.
- Salas, Laura Purdie. *A Rock Can Be...* Minneapolis: Millbrook Press, 2015.
- Wenzel, Brendan. *A Stone Sat Still*. San Francisco: Chronicle Books, 2019.

ASK A LIBRARIAN FOR MORE BOOK RECOMMENDATIONS!

chlorite

arkose

rose quartz

turquoise

feldspar

phyllite

sandstone

calico

gold

magnetite

pink marble

scoria

actinolite

serpentine

jadeite

dolerite

garnet

talc schist

breccia

slate

basalt

sulphur

epidote

corundum

banded gneiss

glauconite

obsidian

mica

amphibole
quartz

graphite

copper

opal

amethyst

olivine

diorite

salt

pyrite

chert

coquina
(shell limestone)

halite

tiger eye

fluorite

soapstone

gypsum

citrine

granite

travertine

pumice

hematite

talc

conglomerate

rhodonite

shale

Text © 2021 by Pat Zietlow Miller
Illustrations © 2021 by Katie Kath
Cover and internal design © 2021 by Sourcebooks
Book design by Chad Beckerman

Watercolor was used to prepare the full color art.

Published by Sourcebooks Jabberwocky, an imprint of Sourcebooks Kids
P.O. Box 4410, Naperville, Illinois 60567−4410
(630) 961-3900
sourcebookskids.com

Library of Congress Cataloging-in-Publication Data is on file with the publisher.

Source of Production: Leo Paper, Heshan City, Guangdong Province, China
Date of Production: June 2021
Run Number: 5021799

Printed and bound in China.
LEO 10 9 8 7 6 5 4 3 2 1